HERE

This one is for all of us
who are from Mars.

SIMON & SCHUSTER BOOKS FOR YOUNG READERS

An imprint of Simon & Schuster Children's Publishing Division

1230 Avenue of the Americas, New York, New York 10020

For information about special discounts for bulk purchases, please contact Simon & Schuster

Special Sales at 1-866-506-1949 or business@simonandschuster.com.

The Simon & Schuster Speakers Bureau can bring authors to your live event. For more

information or to book an event, contact the Simon & Schuster Speakers Bureau at

1-866-248-3049 or visit our website at www.simonspeakers.com.

Book design by Lucy Ruth Cummins

The text for this book is set in Grit Primer.

The illustrations for this book are rendered in pen and ink and watercolor.

Manufactured in China / 0313 SCP

2 4 6 8 10 9 7 5 3 1

Library of Congress Cataloging-in-Publication Data

Kaplan, Bruce Eric.

Cousin Irv from Mars / Bruce Eric Kaplan. — 1st ed.   p. cm.

Summary: Teddy is not looking forward to a visit from Cousin Irv, who comes from

Mars and likes to vaporize things.

ISBN 978-1-4424-4923-7 (hardcover) — ISBN 978-1-4424-4924-4 (eBook)

[1. Cousins—Fiction. 2. Humorous stories.] I. Title.

PZ7.K128973Co 2013   [E]—dc23   2011043872

COUSIN IRV FROM MARS

BRUCE ERIC KAPLAN

SIMON & SCHUSTER BOOKS FOR YOUNG READERS

NEW YORK   LONDON   TORONTO   SYDNEY   NEW DELHI

One day Teddy's mother announced that her cousin Irv was coming to visit. No one in the family had met him before.

"We're not close," she said. "He lives on Mars."

Cousin Irv showed up a few days later.

"Feh," he said to Teddy's mother. "You gave me the worst directions."

She looked at them. "No, I didn't. You wrote them down wrong."

"I forgive you," Cousin Irv said.

"But my leg hurts from being cramped in the saucer.

Plus I've had to go to the bathroom for days."

Teddy's mother showed him where it was.

He was in there for some time.

Then he came out and ate

everything in the kitchen.

In fact, he ate the whole kitchen.

Cousin Irv was exhausted, so he immediately went to bed.

There's nothing worse than having someone stay with you, especially when they put that someone in your room.

On top of which, Cousin Irv breathed really loudly.

So Teddy couldn't fall asleep.

"Is your pillow comfortable?" Cousin Irv asked.

"Yes," Teddy said.

"That's nice," he said. "Mine's a little lumpy."

Cousin Irv was quiet for a moment, then told Teddy how he had gone to many doctors who all said he carried his stress in his neck and needed a comfortable pillow.

"Here." Teddy sighed and threw his pillow over to Cousin Irv.

"You're young," Cousin Irv said as he threw his pillow to Teddy. "You should have a few lumps."

The next day, as Teddy was getting dressed,

Cousin Irv said, "You're not going to school

in *that*?"

"Yes," Teddy said. "What's wrong

with what I'm wearing?"

"Nothing, I suppose," Cousin Irv said.

Teddy sighed and put on a new outfit.

When Teddy came home that

afternoon, he found Cousin Irv

wearing his clothes and playing with

all of his toys.

"I got bored." Cousin Irv

shrugged.

Teddy asked his mother when Cousin Irv was
going home.

She told him people needed to get along with their

distant cousins from Mars.

Teddy tried but he just couldn't, especially because Cousin

Irv listened to the most horrible music.

Life would be so much easier if we all listened to the

same music.

Teddy's parents threw a party for Cousin Irv.

Sadly, every single one of Teddy's relatives came.

Teddy hid in the coats as he always did whenever relatives came over.

Other people's coats make you feel so much safer than your own.

Teddy was angry at Cousin Irv because it was his fault all these people were around.

On the other hand, there was special party food.

If only you could have party food without a party.

The next day Teddy's parents were busy, so they asked Cousin Irv to take Teddy to school.

Teddy pitched a fit.

Teddy's mother explained to Cousin Irv, "Teddy doesn't want you to know that he has no friends at school."

"Those no-goodniks." Irv snorted angrily.

When Teddy and Cousin Irv got to school, everyone gathered around them.

None of them had ever met anyone from Mars.

When the kids started to get bored, Cousin Irv took out his electromagnetic ray and vaporized a few things in the classroom.

The teacher said no electromagnetic rays were allowed in the classroom.

Which of course made Cousin Irv vaporize

everything in the classroom.

From that day on, everyone wanted to be Teddy's friend.

And suddenly Teddy realized he liked Cousin Irv.

You know, if you only see what you don't like about someone, you never see what you do like about them.

For instance, Cousin Irv let Teddy eat pizza in the bath because he didn't know you didn't do that.

When no one was around, Cousin Irv and Teddy would touch everything on Mom and Dad's desk.

There is nothing more wonderful than touching something you're not supposed to touch.

Cousin Irv was happy to read the same book to Teddy

fourteen times in a row.

And Cousin Irv

understood how important

it was to keep piles of

things you never needed in

places you never looked.

At night Teddy could still hear Cousin Irv breathing.

It used to keep him awake.

Now it helped him to go to sleep.

Then one day Cousin Irv said, "Bad news, kid. I have to go home."

"Why?" asked Teddy. "Was it something I did?"

"Not at all," he said. "My petsitter has a better job.

Plus, I just don't like the coffee on Earth."

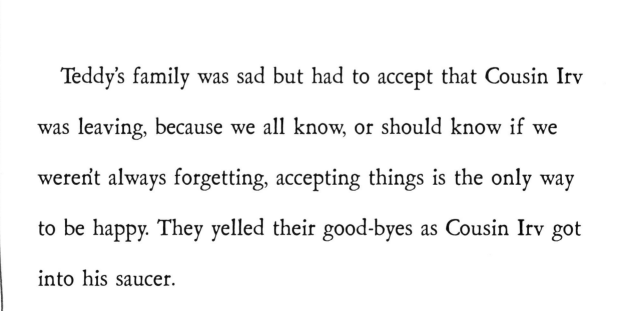

Teddy's family was sad but had to accept that Cousin Irv

was leaving, because we all know, or should know if we

weren't always forgetting, accepting things is the only way

to be happy. They yelled their good-byes as Cousin Irv got

into his saucer.

Then Cousin Irv's saucer wouldn't start.

So they had to wait while it was repaired.

There is nothing more awkward than having to see someone after you've already said good-bye to them.

When the mechanic left, they said good-bye again and Cousin Irv flew back to Mars.

Months passed. Things just weren't the same without Cousin Irv.

Even worse, Teddy's father came home one day and said he got a new job and they had to move. Teddy didn't want to have to make new friends, even though, truthfully, he didn't really like the friends he had.

He was really worried until he learned his dad's new job was

on Mars!

That spring, Teddy and his family moved into Cousin Irv's crater.

Best of all, Teddy went to a great new school, where he made millions of friends.

Teddy loved life on Mars,

except when all of his relatives

from Earth came to visit.

THERE